NTON

## THE BOXCAR CHILDREN MYSTERIES

# THE MYSTERY IN THE SNOW

### created by
## GERTRUDE CHANDLER WARNER

*Illustrated by Charles Tang*

**ALBERT WHITMAN & Company**
Morton Grove, Illinois

ISBN 0-8075-5393-X

3 5 7 9 10 8 6 4 2

Printed in the U.S.A.

# Contents

# CHAPTER 1

# Grandfather's Surprise

Benny glanced out the window over the kitchen counter. Outside, his twelve-year-old sister, Jessie, was playing with their dog, Watch. Snowflakes fell onto the Aldens' back lawn.

"I hope it snows all day," six-year-old Benny said. "And all night!" He dropped the last spoonful of dough onto a cookie sheet.

At the table, his sister Violet, who was ten years old, was sprinkling powdered sugar on a freshly baked batch of golden cookies. "It would be nice to have lots of snow," she said. "We could go sledding."

"And build snowmen," Benny added.

Mrs. McGregor, the Aldens' housekeeper, carried Benny's filled cookie sheet to the oven. "I don't think there's much chance of that," she said. "A few flurries is all those clouds have in them."

Benny sighed. He had been looking forward to the season's first big snowfall. It was late this year. "It won't be much of a winter vacation without snow," he said.

"Let's make our own snow," Violet suggested.

Benny turned away from the window. "How?" he asked.

"We'll cut snowflakes," Violet told him.

Benny knew how to do that. Before vacation, he and the other first-graders had made paper snowflakes to decorate their classroom. "I thought you meant *real* snow," he said, disappointment in his voice.

"We'll hang them in the window, Benny," Violet said. "That way, every time you look out, you'll see snow."

"What a good idea," Mrs. McGregor said.

"And if you make some small snowflakes — no bigger around than the cookies, I'll show you something else you can do."

Benny was curious. He cut the paper into four pieces. Then he folded and refolded each section. In one piece, he cut several small holes. Each was a different shape. When he unfolded the paper, he had a beautiful snowflake.

Mrs. McGregor laid it on top of a cookie.

Violet's eyes lit up. "Talk about good ideas!" she said.

Benny didn't think it was such a good idea. "Who's going to eat cookies with paper snowflakes on them?" he asked.

Mrs. McGregor laughed. "Oh, I think everyone will eat these when we're finished."

Violet sprinkled the powdered sugar over the snowflake. Then she carefully removed the paper. The top of the cookie was dusted with a beautiful white design.

The three of them cut more paper designs.

"Can I sprinkle the sugar?" Benny asked.

Violet handed him the can. Benny turned it upside down and shook hard. The sugar

poured through the holes in the can top like snow from a cloud.

Just then, Jessie opened the door and Watch bolted through. He slid across the floor to the table. Sniffing the air, he sat back on his hind legs and begged. Benny slipped him a cookie.

Jessie hung her coat on the hall tree beside the door. "It sure smells good in here," she said.

Henry, their fourteen-year-old brother, came in with an armload of firewood.

"Is it still snowing?" Violet asked.

Henry set the firewood down near the kitchen fireplace. "It's stopped," he said. "At least *out*side. Looks like a regular snowstorm in here."

Benny laughed. "It's the sugar," he said. "We're using it to make our own snow."

Grandfather Alden entered from the front of the house. He was wearing his overcoat and scarf. His cheeks were rosy and his eyes sparkled. It was early for him to be home. He rarely left his mill until the end of the workday.

"Grandfather!" Benny exclaimed. "What a surprise!"

"Did I hear something about snow when I came in?" Mr. Alden asked.

"We were hoping for a snowstorm," Violet told him.

Grandfather smiled. He looked as though he had a big secret. "What if I said that you'd see more snow this week than you've seen in a very long time?"

"Where?" they all asked at once.

Mr. Alden told them about his friend, Todd Mercer, who owned a lodge in the hills two hours north of Greenfield. "It's a wonderful place," he said. "Every winter holiday, there's a kind of carnival with special events and prizes. Todd's been wanting me to bring you children up there since he bought the lodge."

"Well, then, why haven't you, Grandfather?" Benny asked.

Mr. Alden chuckled. "That's exactly the question I asked myself this morning," he said. "So I phoned Todd."

Benny couldn't stand the suspense. He

shot to his feet. "Are we going?" he asked.

Grandfather looked from one to the other. "Do you want to go?"

They all said, "Yes!"

"When will we leave, Grandfather?" Jessie asked. She was thinking about the packing that would have to be done.

"Do you think you could be ready in" — Mr. Alden looked at his watch — "an hour?"

The children glanced at one another.

Henry wondered if his skis needed waxing.

Jessie wondered if her skates would fit.

Violet wondered where she had put her winter hat — the one with the purple stripes.

Benny wondered what food they would take.

There was so much to do. How could they possibly be ready in an hour? They looked at Grandfather Alden.

"Yes!" they all said. "We'll be ready!"

CHAPTER 2

## *Missing Keys*

Benny was the first to see the carved wooden sign. It read *Snow Haven Lodge*. "We're here!" he exclaimed.

Mr. Alden turned the station wagon into the long driveway. Snowflakes danced in the headlights. "And not a moment too soon," he said. "With all this snow, driving will be impossible before too long."

Violet glanced out her window. The branches of the evergreens were already heavy with snow. The ground below was covered in a soft blanket of white. "It's so beautiful!" she said.

"And so quiet," Jessie said.

"What's that up ahead, Grandfather?" Henry asked. He pointed toward a long, low building. Its lights cast a warm glow through the gathering dusk.

"Must be the lodge," Mr. Alden told him.

"Is that where we'll stay?" Jessie asked.

"I imagine so," Mr. Alden answered.

"I'd rather stay in one of those," Benny said. He pointed to a group of small cabins on their right.

Grandfather stopped the car in front of the lodge. Several other cars were parked there. Watch sat up and wagged his short tail.

They climbed out of the station wagon and headed inside. A fire blazed in the large, stone fireplace. Big, comfortable couches and chairs were grouped on the wood floor. Here and there, small clusters of people talked and laughed.

"James!" A tall, thin man stepped out from behind a counter and came toward them.

Mr. Alden grabbed the man's hand. "Todd, it's good to see you."

Todd Mercer smiled. "I'm glad you made it before the storm," he said.

"So are we!" Benny piped up.

"This must be the famous Benny," Mr. Mercer said.

Benny blushed. He'd never been called *famous* before. It made him speechless.

Mr. Alden introduced his other grandchildren, and Watch, who had followed them inside. "I hope it's all right for our dog to be inside the lodge. He's very well-behaved," said Mr. Alden.

"Fine with me," Mr. Mercer said.

The door opened and a gust of snow blew in. A man and woman dressed in ski suits rushed inside. A rosy-cheeked boy about Henry's age tagged along after them.

"James, why don't you sign in," Mr. Mercer said to Mr. Alden. He turned to the children. "Help yourselves to the hot chocolate and snacks on that table over there." He pointed toward the windows.

Benny's eyes widened when he saw the

table covered with plates of cookies and small sandwiches, and a large, steaming pot of hot chocolate. "What a sight!" he said.

Jessie looked out the windows. Children skated on the pond behind the lodge. Snow fell all around them. "It looks like a picture in a storybook," she said.

"Better," Benny said. "You can't *eat* pictures." He helped himself to a cookie.

Violet laughed. "Oh, Benny," she said. "Jessie was talking about the view."

Benny glanced out the window. "That's nice, too, but — "

"You can't eat it," Henry finished.

They carried their snacks to the couch.

Mr. Mercer brought over the young boy who'd just arrived. "I want you to meet Jimmy Phelps," he said. "He's been with us every winter vacation since he was no bigger than you, Benny."

Jimmy smiled shyly. "Hi," he said.

Henry moved over. "Sit down here," he said. "There's plenty of room."

"Get some food first," Benny suggested. "It's delicious."

Jimmy nodded. "Okay," he said. "And I have to sign in." He went to the high desk and signed the guest book.

Jimmy's parents and Mr. Mercer were talking to Grandfather.

"I wonder if Mr. and Mrs. Phelps are staying here, too," Jessie said.

"Why wouldn't they?" Henry asked.

Jessie shrugged. "Mr. Mercer said Jimmy's been here every winter; he didn't say anything about his parents."

Benny looked at the grown-ups. "Maybe they're not his parents," he said. Just then, Jimmy returned. "Are those people your parents?" Benny asked him.

Jimmy nodded. "Yes," he answered. "Why?"

"Benny asks lots of questions," Henry explained.

"That's the only way to get answers," Benny defended himself.

Everyone laughed.

"Are they staying here, too?" Jessie asked Jimmy.

Jimmy glanced toward his parents. "No,"

he said. "They never stay." He looked glumly at his feet.

"Why not?" Violet asked. "It's such a nice place."

Before he could answer, someone called, "Jimmy!"

Jimmy popped to his feet. "Freddy!"

A girl rushed up. "I am so glad to see you," she said. "I was afraid you wouldn't be here this year."

"Freddy, meet the Aldens," Jimmy said.

"Freddy?" Benny said. "Isn't that a boy's name?"

The girl took off her green knit cap. Her short, black hair curled tightly around her face. "My name's actually Frederica," she said. "Freddy's easier."

"That's for sure," Benny agreed.

Mr. and Mrs. Phelps joined the group.

"Jimmy, we're about ready to go," Mr. Phelps said.

Mrs. Phelps hugged her son. "You're sure you have everything?"

Jimmy sighed. "Mom, how many times did we check?"

"You'll call us if you need anything?" she said.

Mr. Phelps took her arm. "Come on, Grace. With this snow, it'll take us a while to get to the airport." He put his arm around Jimmy. "Walk us out to the car, son," he said.

Freddy watched them leave. When they had gone outside, she said, "They don't know what they're missing."

"Are your parents here?" Jessie asked.

She shook her head. "They went to visit my sister. She moved to Florida last summer. But they'll be here later — for the awards dinner."

"Why didn't you go with them?" Violet wanted to know.

"And miss the snow and the fun here? No way," Freddy said. "Besides, Jimmy and I are team captains this year." She leaned close as though she were about to share a secret. "My team's going to win." She giggled with excitement. "It's going to be the best year ever."

"It'll certainly be the biggest year," Mr.

Mercer said as he came up beside them. "Seems I've overbooked the lodge."

At his side, Grandfather said, "Todd's looking for volunteers to stay in one of those cabins we saw on the way in."

"Anyone interested?" Mr. Mercer asked.

Five hands shot up. Two of them belonged to Benny.

When Jimmy returned, Mr. Mercer called to him. "Jimmy," he said, "I left the team box in the equipment shop. Would you mind getting it? You know where the keys are."

"On the board behind the desk?" Jimmy asked to make sure.

Mr. Mercer nodded.

Jimmy hurried off.

"What's the team box?" Henry asked.

"Everyone signs a card and puts it in the box," Freddy explained. "Tomorrow morning, Jimmy and I will pick names out of it. That's the way we form the teams. Then we have five contests: skiing, sledding, skating, snow sculpting and ice carving."

"Mr. Mercer, I can't find the keys," Jimmy called.

Mr. Mercer went over to help him. The Aldens followed.

Mr. Mercer stepped behind the desk. He looked through the keys hanging on the board. Each one had a tag. "That's strange," he said. "The keys were here earlier today. I put them here myself."

"Maybe they fell on the floor," Jimmy suggested.

Everyone looked around, but no one saw the keys. Mr. Mercer looked upset.

"Couldn't you use another box?" Benny suggested.

"Yes," Mr. Mercer answered, "but we have to be able to get into the equipment shop."

"There're all kinds of things in there we need," Freddy added.

"Without them," Jimmy said, "we won't be able to have the games."

"It will make things very difficult." Mr. Mercer paused a moment. Then, looking around at the concerned faces of all the children he said, "I'm sure they'll turn up *somewhere*."

# CHAPTER 3

# Their Own Little Cabin

After a supper of spaghetti and salad in the lodge dining room, Grandfather drove the children to the cabin.

"This is as close as we can get," he said as he stopped the station wagon.

"We're close enough," Jessie said. "From what Mr. Mercer told me, that's our cabin just over there."

Their log house stood out from the others. It was the only one with a light on.

Everyone hopped out of the car. Watch ran, his nose to the ground. Henry unhooked

the skis from the car's roof. Jessie gathered the skates from the back. Violet, Benny, and Mr. Alden carried the children's suitcases to the cabin. When Grandfather opened the door they all saw a fire dancing in the small stone fireplace with a sofa and two over-stuffed chairs clustered around it. At the end of the room, near a small kitchen, stood a bare table and six plain chairs.

Jessie and Henry came in. They looked around for a place to put their skis and skates. Henry noticed a long wooden board on the wall beside the door.

"This rack must be made for skis," he said. He slipped his skis between two of the metal bands on the board.

"There are pegs here, too," Jessie said. "A perfect place to hang our skates."

"And there's still room for our coats," Violet said as she slipped out of her purple jacket.

They all took off their coats and boots while Grandfather looked around the cabin. He found two small bedrooms, each with bunk beds and a large chest of drawers.

"The beds aren't made," he said when he returned to the main room, "but there are plenty of sheets and blankets in the dresser drawers."

"We'll find everything, Grandfather," Jessie assured him. She knew he wanted to get back to the lodge to visit with Mr. Mercer.

"All right then," Mr. Alden said, "I'll be on my way."

He opened the door and Watch darted in. His nose and whiskers were all white, and snow hung from his chin like a beard. He ran around the room smelling everything, leaving little puddles of melting snow wherever his nose touched.

The Aldens waved to their grandfather. Then, Henry closed and latched the door.

"Benny and I will share one bedroom," he said. "You girls take the other."

"I get the top bunk," Benny said.

"Fine with me," Henry agreed.

Benny unzipped his duffel bag. He pulled out a white box. "What should we do with this?" he asked.

"What's in it?" Jessie asked.

"The cookies we made this morning," Benny answered.

Jessie looked around the room. There was a small sink near the table. Above it was a cabinet. She opened its door. "Put them in here, Benny," she said.

Benny handed her the box. He wasn't tall enough to reach the shelf.

"There're dishes in here and paper napkins. And, look! Here's a tablecloth," Jessie said.

"Let's cover the table," Violet suggested. "It'll look more homey."

Jessie took out the red-and-white checked cloth and laid it on the tabletop.

"Now all we need's a centerpiece," Violet said.

Benny dragged his duffel bag across the room. "How about some fruit?" He put several apples and oranges on the table.

"Here's a container," Henry said. He slipped a basket off a peg beside the fireplace.

Violet arranged the fruit in the round basket and placed it in the center of the table.

Then, Benny said, "Let's eat."

"We just had supper," Henry reminded him.

"I know, but I'm getting sleepy," Benny said, "and I can't go to bed without a snack."

Jessie took down the box of cookies. "I don't suppose a cookie or two would hurt," she said.

"Too bad we don't have something to drink," Violet said.

Benny pulled several cans of juice from his bag. "Ta-da," he said.

Henry laughed. Then, he took four cups from the cabinet shelf.

"I don't need a cup," Benny told him as he fished in the duffel. "I brought my own." He held up the cracked pink cup he had found in a dump when they had lived in the boxcar.

Jessie gave each of them two cookies on a red paper napkin.

Henry poured the juice.

"The juice is warm," Benny said. "I like it cold."

"I can fix that," Henry said. He took a bowl from the cabinet and went outside. He returned with a bowlful of snow.

Benny scooped some into his cup. "It's like a snowcone without the cone," he said.

They began talking about the next day's activities.

"Whose team will we be on?" Violet wondered aloud.

"Maybe we'll be on different teams," Jessie said.

"I want to be on Freddy's team," Benny said.

"Why?" Violet asked. "Jimmy'll be a good captain, too."

"But Freddy said her team was going to win," Benny reminded his sister.

"Just because she says it, doesn't make it so," Jessie argued.

"I don't care who wins," Violet said. "Just being a part of a team will be fun."

"There might not be any teams," Henry said.

They remembered the locked equipment shop.

"What do you suppose happened to the keys?" Jessie asked.

"Maybe someone took them," Benny said.

"Why would anyone do that?" Henry asked.

They could not think of a single reason.

"Maybe Mr. Mercer put them somewhere else and forgot," Violet suggested.

"Let's hope he finds them," Jessie said.

"Or figures out some other way to get into the equipment shop," Henry put in.

Benny shivered with excitement. "I can't wait to find out whose team I'll be on," he said.

They decided to make up their beds and go to sleep. That way, morning would come faster.

CHAPTER 4

## *Flat Tires*

The next morning, the Aldens met Jimmy Phelps in front of the lodge. He was taking off his skates.

"Is breakfast over already?" Benny asked him. He couldn't imagine anyone doing too much before eating.

"No," Jimmy answered. "I was just working up an appetite."

"I'm glad I don't have to do that!" Benny commented.

"Benny likes to eat," Jessie explained.

Jimmy smiled. His rosy cheeks became

even rounder. "I figured that," he said.

On their way into the lounge, Henry asked, "Did Mr. Mercer find the keys?"

Jimmy shook his head. "No," he said. "I don't know what he'll do."

Mr. Mercer stood just inside the door. He pointed to a table near the entrance. "Sign your names on those cards," he said, "and put them into that big box."

"Is that the box from the equipment shop?" Jessie asked.

Mr. Mercer shook his head. "No, the equipment shop is still locked. I'm going into town later to get a locksmith. He can make new keys."

"We thought you might have to call off the games," Henry said.

"Well, it is a problem not being able to get into the equipment shop. But, I'd never call off the games. Not for a little thing like a missing key," Mr. Mercer assured them.

The Aldens went over to fill out the cards.

Their grandfather got up from his chair near the fire. "Good morning," he called out.

"Good morning, Grandfather," the children responded.

Freddy came in, pulling off her green knit hat. She was wearing a one piece ski outfit that was bright green, orange, and yellow. And she had on gloves to match!

"Did everybody sign up?" she called. "I want you all to have a chance to be on my team."

Several children who hadn't filled out the cards formed a line behind the Aldens. Everyone else headed for the dining room. Long tables were set with red-and-white checked tablecloths. At the front of the large, sunlit room, the longest table was filled with food: egg dishes, bacon, sausage, rolls, toast, pancakes, fruit, three kinds of juice, milk, coffee, tea — something for every taste.

"Everything looks so good," Jessie commented. "It's hard to know what to choose."

Benny took a plate from the stack at the end of the table. "Take some of everything," he advised his sister. "That way you won't have to make hard decisions."

Grandfather chose a toasted English muffin and a bowl of fruit; the younger Aldens took Benny's advice.

After breakfast, Mr. Mercer went to the front of the room. Jimmy and Freddy followed with the box of names.

"Attention, everyone," the man said. "It's time to pick teams. Freddy and Jimmy are our team captains. As your name is called, please come up and join your leader."

Everyone started talking excitedly.

Mr. Mercer hushed them. "I have to go into town to the locksmith," he said. "So I'll let your team captains take over." He left the room.

Freddy reached into the box and pulled out a card. "Danny Cahill," she read.

In the far corner of the room, a red-headed boy, about Benny's age, stood up. He walked slowly to the front of the room.

Freddy greeted him with a broad smile. "Welcome to the winning team, Danny," she said.

Jimmy picked out a name. He read it to himself; then looked up. He had a funny expression on his face. It was hard to tell whether he was happy about his choice, or sad. "Beth Markham," he announced. "Last year's top skater."

Beth skipped to the front of the room, her ponytail swinging.

Two more team members were chosen.

Benny wiggled in his chair. "I can't stand the suspense," he whispered.

Henry was the first of the Aldens chosen. He would be on Jimmy's team. Jessie and then Violet were picked for that team, too.

Benny glanced around the room. He and an older girl were the only ones whose names hadn't been called.

It was Jimmy's turn. "There are only two names left," he said.

Benny leaned forward in his chair. "Hurry, hurry, hurry," he urged silently.

Jimmy reached into the box. He drew out a card. He looked at it. He even turned it over.

Benny couldn't sit still. He popped to his feet. "Hurry, hurry, hurry," he repeated, but this time, he said the words aloud.

Everyone laughed. Benny was so embarrassed he sat down again.

Finally, Jimmy said, "And the last member of our team is . . . Benny Alden!"

His new teammates cheered.

Freddy called the last name, "Nan Foster!" and that team cheered as a short girl, who looked like she was about ten years old, slowly walked up. She seemed to be the only person in the room who wasn't smiling.

Just then, Mr. Mercer appeared in the doorway, looking grim. "You're not going to believe this," he said.

"What happened?" Grandfather Alden asked.

"It's my truck. The tires are flat," he responded with disbelief. "All four of them!"

# CHAPTER 5

# A New Mystery

Mr. Mercer was upset. "I parked the truck out by the skating rink last night. The tires were fine then."

"*One* flat tire I could understand," Grandfather said. "But *four*?"

"That sounds like it was intentional," Henry pointed out.

"But who would do something like that? And why?" said Mr. Mercer.

"First missing keys and now flat tires. Do you suppose they're connected?" Henry wondered aloud.

"Probably not," Jessie said.

"Todd, do you have an air pump?" Mr. Alden asked.

Mr. Mercer shook his head. "It's broken," he said. "I've been meaning to get another one."

Grandfather offered to drive him into town. "We'll get a pump *and* go to the locksmith," he said.

Mr. Mercer agreed, and he and Grandfather hurried to Grandfather's car.

Freddy said, "We'll go on with the tryouts."

"There are five events," Jimmy said. "Skating, skiing, sledding, snow sculpting, and ice carving."

An excited murmur shot through the group.

"Snow sculpting?" Benny whispered to Violet. "Is that like making snowmen?"

Violet nodded. "I think so."

"Then, I'll try out for that," he said. He wondered what he would have to do. He raised his hand. "How do you try out for snow sculpting?" he asked.

"You can't," Freddy told him. "That and ice carving — if you want to do one of those, just sign up."

"And you can sign up for as many events as you want," Jimmy added.

A boy about Jessie's age stood up. He tossed his head to get his long, straight hair out of his eyes. "What if you want to try out for, say, skiing, but you don't have skis?"

"You'll find everything you need at the equipment shop, Matt," Freddy told him.

"If and when Mr. Mercer gets it open," Jimmy said.

"What if you don't want to sign up for anything?" Nan Foster asked.

Freddy stared at her. She seemed so surprised by the question that she didn't have an answer.

A boy named Pete, who was sitting next to Nan, rolled his eyes. "We can't win with people like her on our team," he scoffed.

Nan looked as though she might cry.

"It's okay," Jimmy said to her. "Sometimes, people try out for an event, and they don't make it. That's okay, too. They get to be assistants. We need everybody."

Beth smiled at Nan. "You should try out for something, though. It's fun," she said.

"Where do we try out?" Henry asked.

"The skating tryouts are in an hour, at the pond. Right afterward we'll have skiing on the slopes, and then sledding on the smaller hill." Jimmy held up two pieces of yellow lined paper. "Here are the sign-up sheets." He looked around to be sure there were no other questions. "That's it!"

"Yea, team!" Freddy said.

"What're you going to try out for, Henry?" Jessie asked.

"Skiing," Henry answered.

"Anything else?"

"Maybe sledding."

"I'm signing up for ice carving," Violet said. "How about you, Jessie?"

"Skating, for sure," Jessie answered.

"I'm trying out for everything," Benny said.

Henry laughed. "This isn't food, Benny," he teased.

They got in line to sign up.

Violet was behind Nan. "Oh, Nan," she said, "you changed your mind about trying out."

Nan lowered her eyes. "No, I didn't," she said.

Violet was confused. "But . . . you're standing in line."

"I don't want my parents to know," she explained. "They'd be upset. They want me to have fun."

"Don't *you* want to have fun?" Violet asked.

The girl shrugged. "I never have fun," she answered.

Violet thought about that. She tried to imagine what it would be like not to enjoy herself. No matter where she went or what she did, she expected to have a good time. And she always did.

It was Nan's turn to sign up. Twisting the ends of her red knit scarf, she stared at the paper on the table.

Violet stepped up beside her. She picked up two pencils. "Here," she said and gave Nan one. "Let's both sign up for ice carving.

You don't have to try out for that."

Nan looked discouraged. "I don't know anything about ice carving," she said. "I wouldn't want to be the one who loses for the whole team."

"I don't know a thing about it either," Violet assured her. "Maybe we could help each other."

Nan brightened. Then, just as suddenly, her round face clouded. "We're on different teams," she said.

Violet had forgotten that. Because of her brothers and sister, she usually thought about cooperation, not competition. "That won't matter," she said. "It'll be a help just knowing each other. I mean, neither of us knows what we're doing; that makes us equal."

Nan smiled for the first time. "Then, your team'd have an equal chance of losing."

Although Violet wouldn't have put it that way, she agreed.

Nan signed her name on the yellow sheet that read ICE CARVING. "Thanks," she said and hurried off.

When they had all signed up, the children headed back to the cabin to get their skates and skis. Outside, the snow reflected the sunlight.

Henry fished a pair of sunglasses out of his jacket pocket. "It's really bright," he commented.

"I like the way the snow sparkles in places," Violet said.

Benny said, "I like the way it sounds when you walk on it. *Scrunch, scrunch, scrunch.*"

Jessie sighed. She liked everything about the snow. It even made the air smell fresher. "It'll be a good week," she said.

They walked along in silence, each thinking about all that had happened since they had arrived at the lodge.

Finally, Henry said, "You know, I think the missing keys and the flat tires are connected somehow."

"That means we have a mystery," Jessie said.

"I hope you're wrong, Jessie," Benny said. "We'll be too busy to solve one!"

CHAPTER 6

# The Tryouts

A little while later, Benny sat on a bench at the edge of the skating pond. He was trying to lace up his skates. His hands were clumsy inside his gloves. When he took his gloves off, his fingers got too cold. "I'll never get these laces tight enough," he complained aloud.

Jessie was already skating. Henry and Violet had gone to look at the ski run. Benny sighed. There was no one to help him.

From the next bench, an older boy called, "Having trouble?"

It was Matt, the boy with the hair in his eyes. But now, his hair was off his face, held back by a wide black headband.

"It's these laces," Benny said.

Matt walked over on his racing skates. "Here, let me help," he said. Then he bent down and carefully laced up Benny's skates.

"I think these skates may be too small for you," he said.

Benny was surprised. "They fit last year."

Matt laughed. "Well, maybe they shrank," he teased.

"Skates don't shrink," Benny said.

"No, but feet grow."

Benny laughed. "Oh," he said. "I forgot about that."

"You can get a bigger pair at the equipment shop when Mr. Mercer gets new keys," Matt told him. Then, he sped off.

Benny looked at the skaters. Jessie was practicing her forward crossovers. Beth was doing jumps. Jimmy was skating backward. All the people on the ice were excellent skaters. Benny was good, but not that good. He decided not to try out for skating.

Violet and Henry came back in time for the tryouts. Many of the adults came out to the rink to watch the six skaters. Mr. Alden strolled up to the children. He had just returned from driving Mr. Mercer to town.

"The locksmith is making the new keys," he said. "The equipment shop will be open in time for the ski tryouts."

Jimmy put his skaters through their paces quickly. Matt was the best racer; Jessie and Beth the best figure skaters.

Freddy and her group came along. They sat on a bench near the Aldens to put on their skates. Freddy watched Jimmy's skaters carefully. She saw every turn, every pivot, every jump. She did not smile.

"Freddy doesn't look very happy," Benny observed.

Finally, Jimmy was ready to announce his choices. The skaters formed a circle around him.

"Beth, Matt, Jessie, and me." Jimmy pointed to each as he called out their names. To the two losers, he said, "You're both very good. If I could choose more than four skaters, you would have made it, too."

The Aldens admired his kindness.

"Now, there's a good leader," Mr. Alden said.

Jessie skated over.

Everyone congratulated her.

"The ice makes it easy to skate well," she said. "It's smooth as glass."

Freddy stepped onto the ice. "Come on," she said to her group. "Let's show them some real skating." But she still didn't smile.

Grandfather went back to the lodge to warm up. Most of the other adults decided to do that, too.

Jimmy headed for the ski hill. His team trekked along beside him.

"Have you been captain before?" Henry asked.

Jimmy shook his head. "No, this is the first time."

"Do your parents know you're captain?" Jessie asked.

Jimmy looked at her in a strange way. "Why do you want to know?" he asked.

Jessie sensed that she had asked the wrong

question. "Oh, no reason. I just thought if they knew . . ." her voice trailed off.

"I'd want them to be here if I were captain," Benny said.

Jimmy didn't respond.

"Don't you miss them?" Benny persisted. "I miss Grandfather when we're away from him."

Jimmy picked up his pace. "It's only for a week," he said. "And, besides, I like being on my own. Especially here. Who wants parents watching every move you make?"

The Aldens were surprised by his harsh tone. Jimmy had seemed so gentle.

After a brief silence, he added, "Don't get me wrong. My parents are terrific. It's just that they can be . . . overprotective sometimes." His voice had lost its sharp edges.

They came to the ski hill. The run started high above them and ended near a long, low, log building.

"Wow!" Benny exclaimed. "That's no hill! It's a mountain."

"It looks like great skiing," Henry commented.

Jimmy shrugged. "It's not bad, but it's nothing compared to the runs in Colorado. That's where my parents are."

"How do you get to the top?" Benny asked.

"Rope tow," Jimmy said. He pointed to a rope moving slowly up the incline.

To Benny, it looked like a moving snake. He trudged along behind his brother toward the log building. It housed the equipment shop and a warming room.

Mr. Mercer was just leaving. "The equipment shop is open," he said.

People clumped across the wooden floor in colorful plastic boots. Dressed in ski clothes and goggles, they looked like moon walkers — only clumsier.

Benny doubted he could walk in the boots, let alone ski. "I don't think I'll try out for skiing," he said.

"That's a good decision," Henry told him. "It's a tough run for a beginner."

"But I would like to try it," Benny said.

"Maybe you could take a lesson," Henry said, changing into his boots. "See you later."

"Good luck!" Benny called out.

Henry went outside. There he snapped on his skis and glided toward the other skiers.

Benny joined his sisters near the windows in the warming house.

"Did you change your mind about trying out?" Jessie asked.

Benny nodded. "I need my energy for snow sculpting."

Violet held up the book she was reading. "You might want to look at this," she said. "It's tells all about ice carving and snow sculpting. I found it in the equipment shop."

"I know how to build snowmen," Benny said.

"But you can build all kinds of other things, too," Violet told him. "It doesn't have to be a snowman."

Benny sat down beside her to look at the book. There were lots of photographs and instructions. You could make lions, dragons, castles — anything. "I still think I'll build a snowman," he said.

They all moved closer to the windows to watch Henry coming down the slope. From this distance, the skiers looked like small, dark shapes. It wasn't long, though, before they spotted Henry. In his bright red ski jacket, he led the pack.

The Aldens weren't surprised when their big brother came inside all smiles, saying, "I made it!"

The sledding tryouts were held on a smaller hill. Everyone who tried out made it. Benny and some of the younger team members would use round plastic sleds. Henry and the other older children would be on toboggans.

That decided, Jimmy said it was time for lunch.

Benny wasn't the only one who was happy to hear that.

# CHAPTER 7

# *The Competition Begins*

The Aldens had just sat down to eat when Pete burst into the dining room. He was wearing large orange boots. Their thick rubber soles left a line of snow stars on the floor as he stormed along.

Freddy followed after him. She pulled off her orange, green, and yellow gloves and stuffed them into her pockets. "Pete, listen to me," she said. "You can be timekeeper. That's an important job."

Pete rolled his eyes. "I don't want to be

timekeeper!" he shouted. "I don't want to be anything!" He stormed off.

Jimmy came along carrying his lunch tray. "What's the matter with Pete?" he asked Freddy.

"He didn't make the events he wanted." She moved close to Jimmy and lowered her voice. "This whole thing — it's not fair," she hissed. "You got all the good people. Something has to be done. Something to . . . even things out."

She noticed the Aldens watching her. She turned to them and smiled. "Oh, hi," she said, her tone bright. "I was just telling Jimmy that next year, we'll have to divide up families. It's not fair that one team gets all that talent." She sailed off toward the buffet table.

Jimmy sat down. "We do have a good team," he said. "We could win."

"Are your parents coming for the awards dinner?" Benny asked.

Jimmy's entire face turned red as his cheeks. "The awards dinner? I — uh — "

"Freddy told us about it," Henry said.

"She told us her parents were coming," Benny said. "Will yours be here?"

Jimmy stood up abruptly. "They wouldn't miss it," he said. He took his tray and moved on.

"I wonder why he rushed off like that?" Violet said.

"Maybe he didn't want to talk about the awards dinner," Henry said.

"Why wouldn't he?" Jessie wondered.

Henry shrugged. "The competition hasn't even started. Maybe he thinks it's bad luck to talk about awards so soon."

"Pete and Freddy seemed upset, too," Violet reminded them.

"I'm not sure I like this competition business," Benny said. "It makes everybody act funny."

"You can't think about competing," Jessie told him. "Just think about doing the best you can."

After lunch, Benny met with the other sculptors out on the lawn in front of the lodge. They were all about the same age. The only things they had made with snow were balls, forts, and people.

"We should stick to something that's not too hard," Benny decided.

The others — Jason, Alan, and Debbie — agreed. They would build snowpeople. But what kind?

"Why not do *us*?" Alan asked. "We could have them — us — working on a snow sculpture."

"That's a great idea!" Benny said.

Violet's ice carving group — Violet, Beth, and David — were meeting near the ski slope. No one had ever carved ice before. They were all afraid they couldn't do it.

"It will have to be a simple shape," Beth said.

Watch ambled over to the group. He yawned and put his head in Violet's lap. That gave her an idea.

"How about a dog?" she asked. "We could use Watch as a model."

Beth twisted her pony tail around her fingers. "The legs would be hard to carve," she said.

Violet thought about that. Then, she said, "We won't have to worry about the back legs if we're making him sit."

At the sound of the word *sit*, Watch perked up his ears. Then, he sat.

Everyone laughed.

Benny and his group were having problems. They tried rolling the snow into bigger and bigger balls, but chunks kept falling off.

"The snow's too powdery," Jason complained.

Benny had an idea. "If we had some pans, we could fill them with water and pour it on the snow," he said. "That'd make it easy to pack."

They got four buckets of water from the kitchen. Then, they poured the water on the snow. At first, it seemed as though Benny's plan would work. But the water went fast.

Jason sighed. "We can't keep going all the way back to the kitchen."

"Even if we had enough water," Alan said, "the snow would be too heavy to roll."

"Then we'll have to find some other

way to build," Debbie said.

"Like what?" Jason asked.

Benny remembered a picture he had seen in the snow-sculpting book. "If we had some sticks or something, we could build forms," he said.

Alan liked the idea. "It'll be easy to pack the snow around them," he said.

They looked for something to use to make forms. Behind the lodge, they found a scrap heap next to the garage. Debbie saw an old sled under a tarpaulin. They piled it with metal pipes and strips of wood.

"Take that wire, too," Benny said. "It's perfect for holding the form together."

Now that they knew what they were doing, the work went fast. In an hour, four stick figures stood in the snow. By supper time, they had the rough beginnings of snowy self-portraits.

"I wonder how Freddy's team is doing," Jason said.

"Don't worry about them," Benny said. "Just think about doing the best we can."

# CHAPTER 8

# Smashed Snowmen

At 5:30, the snow sculptors were too cold and tired to work anymore. Benny hurried inside to the dining room, where he spotted his sisters and brother at a table. He rushed over to join them. "Wait till you see our snowpeople!" he said.

Pete stomped into the dining room. He sat down at a corner table.

Henry pushed himself away from the table. "I think I'll ask him to eat with us," he said.

"He still looks pretty angry," Benny commented.

"Maybe we can cheer him up. He seemed so unhappy at lunch," Jessie said.

Henry went over and sat down next to Pete. "We have room at our table," he said.

"So?" Pete snapped.

Henry shrugged. "We thought you might like to eat with us."

Pete rolled his eyes. "You thought wrong."

Henry stood up. "Well, if you change your mind . . ."

Violet knew Henry felt bad. When he returned to their table, she said, "Maybe he'll eat with us tomorrow."

"Where's Grandfather?" Benny asked. "I want to show him our snowpeople."

"He's eating later, with Mr. Mercer," Violet told him.

"I'd like to tell Jimmy about them, too," Benny said, looking around. "Where is he?"

"I don't think he's here yet," Jessie said.

"Freddy hasn't come in either," Henry added.

Mr. Mercer's helper filled plates with hamburgers and French fries and passed them down the table.

"My favorite!" Benny exclaimed.

Jessie laughed. "Everything's your favorite, Benny," she teased.

Pete ate fast and started out of the room.

"Looks like Pete's not staying for dessert," Henry observed.

"He's not even staying for second helpings," Benny put in.

Shortly after Pete left, Freddy appeared. She went from table to table asking, "Has anyone seen my glove?"

When she asked the Aldens, Benny said, "They're in your pocket."

Freddy yanked out an orange, green, and yellow glove. "The other one," she explained. "I lost it somewhere."

Jessie remembered seeing her with both gloves at lunch. "Maybe one fell on the floor," she said.

They looked all around. Benny looked under the table. No glove.

"Good thing I have another pair," Freddy said.

She stuffed the glove back into her pocket. Something fell to the floor. Freddy scooped it up quickly, but the Aldens saw it.

It was a key, with a tag attached to it.

Freddy hurried away without looking at the Aldens.

Behind the Aldens, someone asked, "What was all that about?"

It was Jimmy.

"Freddy lost a glove," Violet told him.

He shrugged. "It'll turn up."

"And she had a key," Violet said. "I wonder if it's the one Mr. Mercer's missing."

Jimmy shook his head. "Probably her room key."

"She picked it up so fast," Jessie said. "Like she didn't want anyone to see it."

Jimmy waved that away. "Freddy does everything fast," he said.

Benny told him about the snow sculpture. "Will you come and see it after supper?" he asked.

"I won't have time," Jimmy said. "I have to call my parents and take care of some things for tomorrow. I'll see it in the morning."

"Okay," Benny said. "By then we'll have even more work finished."

He didn't sound disappointed, but the other Aldens knew he was.

"Can *we* see your masterpiece?" Henry asked.

Benny brightened. "Let's go!"

Jessie laughed. "Aren't you forgetting something, Benny?"

Benny was puzzled.

"Dessert!" Jessie, Violet, and Henry said all together.

Benny glanced around. People were still eating their hamburgers.

"We'll be back in time," he assured them.

They trooped out of the dining room and into the lounge, where Watch was lying by the fire. He joined the parade. Benny led them all outside, down the stairs, and across the lawn. It was dark, but floodlights poured bright pools onto the snow.

Nearly running now, Benny said, "It's around the side." When he turned the corner, he saw a long shadow disappearing behind the lodge.

Watch began to bark.

"Quiet, boy," Jessie directed. "Everything's all right."

But as she and Henry and Violet came up beside Benny, Jessie knew she had spoken too soon.

Chunks of snow were scattered everywhere. Two of the forms were completely bare. Pieces of wood and bits of pipe stuck out from the other snowpeople like broken bones.

Watch ran around, sniffing and barking.

"Our snowpeople!" Benny said, stunned. "What happened?"

No one had an answer.

# CHAPTER 9

# Tracks

The Aldens stood close together, silently looking at the fallen snow figures.

Henry put an arm around Benny's shoulder. "Maybe it was an accident," he said, hoping to comfort his brother.

Benny didn't respond.

"What kind of accident?" Violet asked.

Henry shrugged. "Not an accident exactly," he answered. "What I mean is, maybe an animal did it. A raccoon or something."

Benny shook his head. "A person did it,"

he said angrily. "On purpose. I just know it."

Jessie saw something on the path beside the snow sculptures. She squatted down for a better look. "Benny's right," she said. "Look at these."

"They're tracks," Violet said.

"*Boot* tracks," Henry added.

Benny knelt down on the snow. "Pete's boots," he said.

"How can you tell?" Henry asked.

"Look at the pattern," Benny said. "It's the same as the one Pete's boots made in the dining room at lunch."

Violet searched her memory. Pete's large orange boots did leave a pattern of snow on the wood floor. "Stars," she remembered.

Henry examined the print. The star shapes were barely visible outlines on the surface of the snow. Other shapes stood out more. It was the reverse of the pattern on the floor.

"The stars on the boot must be indented — sort of like cookie cutters," he said.

"So the snow packs into them and drops out later," Jessie concluded.

"Pete did it," Benny said.

"You can't be sure, Benny," Violet said. "There could be other people with boots like that."

"He left the dining room early, didn't he?" Benny argued. "And I saw him out here."

Henry was surprised. "You saw him?"

Jessie asked, "When?" and Violet, "Where?"

Benny pointed toward the back of the lodge. "He was just going around that corner when we came out here."

"You're sure it was Pete?" Henry asked. "It's pretty dark out here. Could it have been someone else?"

Benny shook his head. "It was Pete's shadow," he said.

"Pete's shadow?" Violet repeated.

"If it was only a shadow, Benny, you can't be sure it was Pete," Jessie said.

"Let's go back to the lodge, and think this through," Henry suggested.

"I'm too upset to think," Benny said.

"Are you too upset to have dessert?" Violet asked.

Benny sighed. "I suppose I could eat a little."

Henry chuckled. "That's our Benny," he said.

Benny found his teammates Jason, Alan, and Debbie in the lounge. He told them what had happened, but he didn't mention Pete. They raced outside to see for themselves.

Pete was not in the lounge or the dining room.

"He's probably hiding," Benny decided.

The Aldens picked up their dessert plates from the front table and sat down to eat. Watch lay down at Jessie's feet.

"Why would Pete do such a thing?" Henry wondered aloud.

"He's angry because he has to be time-keeper," Violet said.

"But he's on *Freddy's* team," Jessie reminded them. "Wouldn't he want to get back at her?"

"Maybe he ruined their snow sculptures, too," Benny put in.

That was possible. They decided to check.

"But first," Benny suggested, "we should all have a second piece of pie."

Jason, Alan, and Debbie came rushing up to the Aldens' table.

"We know who did it!" Jason told Benny.

Benny looked up at him. "So do I," he said.

"That dog of yours," Jason said.

The Aldens looked at each other in disbelief.

"Watch did it all right," Debbie said.

"What makes you think that?" Henry asked.

"The tracks," Alan said.

"We saw dog tracks," Debbie added.

"It had to be Watch," Jason concluded. "He's the only dog here."

Watch lowered his head and scooted under the table.

# CHAPTER 10

# Another Clue

Watch destroying the snow-people? The idea made Henry laugh.

"Watch wouldn't do that," he said.

Benny was angry. "He *didn't* do it," he said. "He was in the lounge the whole time." Benny reached under the table and patted Watch's head.

"Then how'd the tracks get there?" Jason challenged.

"We took Watch with us when we went out to see your snow sculpture," Violet explained.

"He went wild," Jessie added. "He ran around sniffing and barking. He knew something was wrong."

"If Watch didn't do it, who did?" Debbie asked.

"I'll bet Watch knows," Benny said.

"That's silly," Jason said.

"He's right," defended Violet. "Dogs' noses are sensitive. Watch must have picked up the scent. He knows who did it."

"A lot of good that does us," Jason said.

"Did you see any other tracks out there?" Benny asked. He wanted to know if they had seen Pete's boot prints.

"There were tracks all over the place," Alan said.

"Lots of different tracks," Jason put in.

Benny's eyes widened. The only tracks he had seen were Pete's. "Whose were they?" he asked.

Henry laughed. "They were probably ours, Benny."

"Oh, right," Benny said. "I forgot about that."

Jason sank to a chair. "What're we going

to do now?" he asked. "We don't have a chance of winning."

"The judging isn't until tomorrow afternoon," Jessie said.

"But there's so much work," Jason argued.

Debbie sighed. "At least the forms are there. They weren't destroyed."

"And we have all morning to work," Alan said.

"Why don't we meet early?" Benny suggested.

"That's a good idea," Debbie agreed.

"Before breakfast," Alan said.

"*Before* breakfast?" Benny repeated. He hadn't meant *that* early.

"It's the only way we have a chance of finishing," Alan argued.

Alan was right, they finally decided.

The Aldens took their plates to the kitchen. Then, they went to check on the other snow sculpture. Watch padded along beside them.

Freddy's snow builders had not made much progress. It was hard to tell what the sculpture would be. But it was easy to see that no damage had been done to it.

Benny still thought that Pete was guilty.

"But Pete's angry at *Freddy*, not Jimmy," Jessie said, repeating her earlier doubt.

"Maybe he's acting," Violet suggested. "Maybe Pete is only pretending to be angry at Freddy."

"Why would he do that?" Henry asked.

"To throw everybody off the track," Violet said.

Benny shook his head. "I don't get it."

"Suppose Pete really wants Freddy's team to win, but he doesn't think they have a chance," Violet explained.

"He might do anything to make sure the team wins. Is that what you're saying, Violet?" Jessie asked.

Violet nodded. "If he acts as if he doesn't care about his team, no one will suspect him."

"If Pete had a plan like that, he would have remembered to cover his footprints," Jessie said.

"And what about the missing keys and the

flat tires?" Henry said. "I think they're all connected."

"Let's go back to Benny's snowpeople," Violet suggested. "We might see something we missed."

At the site, Watch ran this way and that, sniffing as he had before. Benny searched for Pete's boot prints, but they were gone, covered over by other tracks.

"Our evidence has disappeared," he said.

Watch stopped beside a large chunk of snow. He sniffed. He scratched.

"What is it, Watch?" Jessie asked.

The dog kept scratching at the snow. Finally, he grabbed something orange, green, and yellow in his mouth, trotted over, and dropped it at Jessie's feet.

"It's a glove!" Violet identified.

"It's *Freddy's* glove!" Jessie said.

# CHAPTER 11

# A Fresh Start

The Aldens trudged back to the cabin silently. Each was deep in thought. Finding the glove in the snow near the smashed sculpture was a shock. It belonged to Freddy; that much, they knew. But they weren't sure what it meant.

In the cabin, Jessie put Freddy's glove on the table. Henry made a fire. Violet and Benny changed into their flannel pajamas. Then, they all settled close to the fireplace.

Finally, Benny spoke. "Now, we have two clues."

"Pointing in different directions," Henry said.

"Pete could have put Freddy's glove in the snow to make it look like *she* did it," Violet said.

"If he did that, wouldn't he remember to cover his tracks?" Henry said. He shook his head. "I don't think he did it. His prints don't mean any more than Watch's do."

"Do you think Freddy did it?" Benny asked.

Henry shrugged. "I don't know."

"She wants to win, that's for sure," Violet said.

They had all heard Freddy's conversation with Jimmy. She thought Jimmy's team was better. "Something has to be done to even things out," they remembered her saying. Perhaps ruining the snowpeople was her way of doing just that.

"She came in late to supper," Jessie remembered.

"And she was looking for her glove," Benny added. "She could have smashed the snowpeople while we were eating."

"If I had just done that, and my glove was missing, I'd go back to look for it," Henry reasoned. "I wouldn't tell everyone I'd lost it."

Benny yawned. "We'll never figure this one out," he said.

"What we need's a good night's sleep," Jessie said.

"Yes," Violet said. "Tomorrow they're judging the snow sculptures, and then come the ski races."

"We'll make a fresh start in the morning," Henry said.

Benny awoke at dawn. He dressed quickly and quietly, then slipped four apples into his pockets and started out. Watch followed him.

"All right, boy," Benny whispered. "You can come with me."

Outside, Watch took off on the run, his short tail wagging.

"Wait up!" Benny called. He hurried along the path behind foggy bursts of his breath.

Alan, Debbie, and Jason were already

hard at work. They had repaired one snow-person and were working on another.

"What should *I* do?" Benny asked.

"You can patch Debbie's arms," Alan answered.

Benny grinned. "Her arms look fine to me," he joked.

They all laughed.

They worked well together, much faster and better than they had the day before.

When they were half finished, Benny remembered how hungry he was. "Who wants an apple?" he asked.

Everyone did. They stood back to admire their work, and munched the crisp, tart apples.

"What will we do at breakfast time?" Jason asked. "We can't leave our snow sculpture alone."

Alan nodded. "That's right. Someone might come along and wreck everything again."

"We can take turns guarding," Debbie suggested.

Benny broke off a piece of apple and gave

it to Watch. "I have a better idea," he said. "We can leave Watch here. He's a good guard dog."

That decided, they got back to work.

At breakfast, Benny asked Violet, "What did you do with Freddy's glove?"

"We brought it with us," Violet answered. "Jessie has it."

"We're going to give it back to her," Henry said.

"We won't have any evidence then," Benny objected.

"The glove doesn't really prove anything, Benny," Jessie said. "And we might be able to tell something from the way Freddy reacts when we give it back to her."

They were on their way out the lodge door when Freddy came in with members of her team. Her smile melted when she saw the Aldens.

"Oh, Benny," she said, "I just heard about what happened yesterday. I'm really sorry."

Benny didn't respond. He didn't think she was at all sorry.

Jessie pulled the glove out of her pocket. "Freddy, we found this. I think it belongs to you."

Freddy took the outstretched glove. "Great!" she said. "Thanks."

"Don't you want to know *where* we found it?" Benny asked.

Freddy shrugged. "If you want to tell me," she answered.

Benny opened his mouth to speak, but Henry spoke first. "It was in the snow," he said.

Freddy nodded. "It wasn't in here," she said. "It had to be outside somewhere."

Violet said, "We found it near — "

"I'm sorry — I've got to go," Freddy interrupted. "I just remembered we have some planning to do." She added, "Victory speeches," and then she hurried away.

# CHAPTER 12

# Missing Skis

By mid-morning, Benny's team had finished their work.

"We did it!" Alan said. He smiled at the finished snowpeople.

Even Jason smiled. "I never thought we'd get done."

Benny walked around the four snowpeople. "They're good, all right," he said. "But will anyone know they're supposed to be us?"

Everyone agreed he had a point. The snow statues needed something more.

Jason took off his baseball cap and set it

on top of his snow self. "How's that?" he asked.

"Perfect!" Debbie exclaimed.

"I have an extra pair of glasses in my room," Alan said. "I could use those."

Debbie didn't know what to add. Finally, she came up with an idea: skates. "I'll put them beside her," she said.

It was Benny's turn. He tried to think of something that no one but he would have. "Oh, I know," he said at last. "My pink cup. It's back at our cabin."

Alan ran off to his room for his spare glasses, and Benny went back to the cabin for the cup. With those things in place, their sculpture was complete.

Benny and Jason smoothed away their footprints. Alan and Debbie took the water buckets back to the kitchen.

They left Watch to guard their snowpeople until judging time.

Benny hurried off to find Henry. There was time for a ski lesson. Along the way, he saw Violet, working with her ice-carving team.

"How're you doing?" he asked.

Violet shook her head. "It's hard," she said. "The ice breaks so easily."

"I'm glad I was working with snow!" Benny said.

He continued on to the ski slope. He found Jimmy in the warming house, by the fire.

"Wait till you see our snowpeople," Benny told him.

Jimmy looked surprised. "You finished?"

Benny nodded. "We didn't think we'd make it," he said.

"I heard someone wrecked your sculptures," Jimmy said. "I figured we'd have to cancel your event."

"We're going to win," Benny assured him.

Jimmy got to his feet. "I hope so," he said, but he didn't sound very hopeful.

Benny shrugged and went back outside.

Henry swooped down the slope toward him. Inches from Benny, he turned his skis to the side and came to a perfect stop. Snow sprayed everywhere.

"Can you teach me that?" Benny asked eagerly.

Henry laughed. "You have to learn to start before you can learn to stop," he said.

At lunchtime, everyone was excited. They seemed to have forgotten about the smashed sculptures and the missing keys and the flat tires. The talk was about the judging.

Nan stopped at the Aldens' table. "Violet," she said, "you should see our ice carving!" It was the first time they had seen her smile in a while.

"We're having a hard time with ours," Violet told her.

"Oh, it's hard work," Nan agreed, "but it's such fun! I'm so glad you encouraged me to sign up."

Pete stomped by in his orange boots and electric-blue earmuffs.

"Pete!" Henry called, but the boy didn't hear him.

After lunch, Mr. Mercer announced the judges' names. A group of four adults would decide each event. Grandfather couldn't be a judge because he had grandchildren in every event.

"But I'll be there cheering you on," he said.

"We will too," said Violet.

Benny said, "See you later," and went outside to wait with his team for the judging.

It was a long wait, or so it seemed. Finally, the judges appeared, followed by the spectators. Each judge carried a clipboard. First they looked at Freddy's team's sculpture, which was a huge igloo.

"Wow," Benny said. "That's great."

Then they all walked over to where Benny's team had worked. The judges walked around the snow people, nodding and making notes. No one spoke.

Finally, one said, "We have all we need."

"You've done a good job," another said.

Benny couldn't stand the suspense. "But did we win?" he asked.

"We won't know until we add the scores," a judge answered.

"And you won't know until the awards dinner," another said.

Benny and his teammates groaned. All the work they had done and redone seemed like nothing. Waiting was much harder.

After the snow sculptures were judged,
everyone gathered at the ski hill. The first
race was about to begin. Jimmy and Freddy
were giving last minute instructions. The
team members would ski down the hill one
by one. Each skier's time would be recorded.
The results would be added together for the
team's final score.

"You can do it," Freddy told her team.
"You *have* to do it."

"One minute, thirty-two and one-half seconds," Pete said and held up a stopwatch.
He had been practicing for his job as timekeeper by timing Freddy's speech.

The Aldens stood near Jimmy's team.
Matt was not there.

"We'll have to start without him," Jimmy
said.

"But he's our best skier," someone protested.

Jimmy nodded. "I know. Without him, we
can't win."

"We can try our best," Henry said.

Freddy marched over. Instead of her green hat, she wore a purple headband. "Are you ready or what?" she asked impatiently.

"We're one member short," Jimmy said. "Maybe we should just forget about the race. We don't have a chance."

Just then, Matt came out of the warming house. He ran over, his hair flopping in his face. "My skis are missing!" he announced.

Benny shot Jessie a glance. "Someone took his skis!"

"I left them over there right before breakfast," Matt said. He pointed to a rack near the warming house.

"Did you check the equipment shop?" Jimmy asked. "Maybe someone put them back in there."

Matt shook his head. "They're not there."

"Can't you borrow another pair?" Henry asked.

Matt shrugged. "That was the only pair my size."

"Use a longer pair," Henry suggested. "They're faster."

Matt tossed the hair out of his eyes. "But

they aren't as easy to control, and there's no time to practice."

Freddy shifted from one foot to the other. "So are you going to ski?" she asked Matt.

"I'll ski last," he said. "That will give me time to keep looking." He turned and ran toward the warming house.

The other skiers grabbed onto the tow and were pulled up the hill.

"Let's go look around," Benny suggested to his sisters. "Maybe we can find out what happened to Matt's skis."

He and the girls hurried to the rack where Matt had left his skis. There were tracks everywhere.

"Everyone leaves skis here," Jessie said. "We'll never be able to tell anything from the footprints."

They searched the ground, but there was no clue of any kind.

"Maybe someone took Matt's skis by mistake," Violet said.

Jessie looked doubtful. "First snow sculptures and now this. Someone doesn't want our team to win," she said.

Then they heard Mr. Alden call, "Henry's skiing next."

Jessie, Benny, and Violet ran back to watch. Freddy was just finishing her run.

"That purple headband she's wearing doesn't go with her outfit," Jessie commented.

"It's a pretty color, though," Violet said.

High above them, Henry was poised for his run. The timekeeper raised a flag, counted to three, then lowered it. The skier was off, bombing down the hill, straight for them.

The Aldens jumped up and down excitedly. "Come on, Henry!" they shouted.

When Henry reached the bottom, he came to a stop.

"Good run," the timekeeper said.

Freddy's last racer skied well.

Matt came trudging back just in time. He was wearing a pair of skis that he'd borrowed. "They're not the right length," he said, "but they'll have to do."

He skied well after all, and the whole team cheered.

There was a break before the second race. Mr. Alden took Watch for a walk. Henry snapped off his skis and headed for the rack. Jessie, Violet, and Benny walked along beside him.

"I sure hope Matt's skis turn up," Henry said.

The next race was a slalom. The team members would have to maneuver around four poles set along the slope. If a skier wasn't used to his skis, it could be especially difficult.

"We think someone took Matt's skis to keep him from racing," Benny said.

"I wonder. There have been a lot of strange things going on," Henry said, leaning his skis against the rack. Just then, something caught his eye. "What's that over there?" he asked.

They walked over to a tall juniper. There was something hung on a lower branch. It was Freddy's green knit cap!

# CHAPTER 13

# Too Many Suspects

Henry picked the green knit hat off the tree branch. "It's Freddy's all right," he said.

"She took Matt's skis!" Benny exclaimed.

"She might have hid them somewhere," Jessie reasoned. "Her hat must have gotten stuck on the branch as she passed by."

"But she'd have known it had gotten stuck," Henry said. "She'd feel it."

"Not if she was in a hurry," Violet argued.

Benny nodded. "She was probably scared someone would see her."

"Remember, we also found her glove near the snow sculptures," Henry said.

"But she didn't act at all guilty when we gave it back to her," Violet said.

That was true. And confusing. They had expected more of a reaction.

"She didn't even want to know where we found the glove," Jessie said.

"That's because she knew where we found it," Benny said.

A whistle sounded. The slalom race was about to begin.

Henry stuffed the cap in his pocket. "It'll take a lot more than a glove and a hat to figure out this mystery," he said. He snapped on his skis and glided toward the hill.

It was Freddy's turn, but Pete wasn't ready to clock her. His earmuffs were missing. "I put them right here on the bench," he complained loudly.

Someone volunteered to look for them while he did his job. Finally, he flagged Freddy and started the stopwatch. Her team skied very well.

"Do you suppose someone took Pete's ear-

muffs?" Benny wondered aloud.

"There are certainly a lot of things missing lately," Jessie said.

"Look," Violet said. "Our team is skiing now."

Jimmy didn't do very well. He skipped one pole and knocked over another. He left the ski hill after his run. Matt cleared the poles, but he was slow. Henry made up for lost points.

The Aldens started for the lodge.

Freddy caught up with them. "Is that my hat sticking out of your pocket?" she asked Henry.

Henry pulled it out and handed it to her.

Saying, "Thanks," she took off the headband and put on the hat. "Where'd you find it?" she asked.

As Henry was about to answer her, Jimmy approached from the opposite direction. He was carrying a pail.

"Where are you going with that?" Freddy called.

Jimmy dropped the pail into the snow. "I'm returning it to the kitchen," he said.

"Someone left it out by our snow sculpture."

Benny was surprised. "I thought Alan and Debbie took our buckets back," he said.

Jimmy shrugged. "They must've forgotten one. Unless someone else left it there . . ."

With so much going on this morning, that was certainly possible.

"What happened, Jimmy?" Freddy asked. "You blew the slalom."

Jimmy's cheeks reddened. "I know. I was really mad at myself. I guess I was worried about Matt — how he would do."

"That's too bad," Freddy said. "But good for my team. Look, they found my hat. Every time I lose something, the Aldens find it. Pretty suspicious if you ask me." Her tone was light and her eyes twinkled.

It made Benny mad. She was the guilty one. How could she accuse them of anything?

Freddy leaned over and picked up the bucket. "Come on, Jimmy," she said, "I'll walk you to the kitchen. We've hardly had any time to talk."

As soon as they were gone, Benny said,

"How could she accuse us that way?"

"She was only joking, Benny," Violet said.

"She has a point, though," Henry said. "If she isn't guilty, it must look strange to her. First we find her glove, and then I'm walking around with her hat in my pocket."

"She's guilty all right," Benny said.

"Watch didn't destroy your snow sculptures," Jessie reminded him. "But your friends thought he did."

"And for a while you were sure Pete did it," Henry said.

Violet sighed. The more she thought about this puzzle the more confusing it became. "Is there anything we can be sure of?" she asked.

"I'm sure of one thing," Benny answered. "I can't think another thought until I have something to eat."

# CHAPTER 14

# More Mischief

Inside the lodge, the Aldens got cups of hot chocolate and cinnamon buns and sat down by the fire.

Grandfather and Mr. Mercer came in.

"Congratulations, Henry," Mr. Mercer said. "You skied well."

"Thank you," Henry said.

"And, Benny, your snow sculpture is something to see."

Benny smiled, but Grandfather could tell something was troubling him.

"What's wrong, Benny?" Grandfather asked.

"Someone's trying to keep our team from winning," Benny blurted.

Mr. Mercer's dark eyes narrowed. "Is that so?"

"It looks that way," Henry said.

Mr. Alden sank into a chair. "We heard there was some trouble with the snow sculptures, but . . ." his voice trailed off.

"And someone took Matt's skis to keep him from doing his best," Benny said.

Mr. Mercer shook his head. "Jimmy said something at breakfast about missing skis. He wanted me to call off the race. I thought they'd turn up — that they were just misplaced." He paused. "Who could do such a thing?" he wondered.

"So many things have been going wrong — even the missing keys and the flat tires," Henry said.

"But they have nothing to do with your team," Mr. Alden said.

Henry nodded. "That's why this mystery is so confusing."

Just then, there was a commotion at the door. Nan and Pete were shouting at each other and tugging at something.

"Here, here. What's going on?" Mr. Mercer called.

Nan and Pete marched over. Each had hold of one of Pete's blue earmuffs. They were tugging so hard that the metal connecting band was stretched to its limit.

"She won't give me my earmuffs!" Pete complained.

"He ruined our ice carving!" Nan snapped. "We were making a castle. Now, the tower's gone." She wiped her tears with her red scarf. "Pete did it," she concluded. "We found his earmuffs right there in the snow."

Pete rolled his eyes. "I didn't do it," he defended. "Someone *took* my earmuffs."

The Aldens exchanged disbelieving glances. Now, the mischief was aimed at *both* teams.

Everyone trekked outside to look at the ice carving Freddy's team had made. The entire castle tower had melted away.

"The sun didn't do it," Mr. Mercer decided. "It doesn't work that fast."

"I didn't do it, either," Pete said.

The Aldens thought he was telling the truth. He was too busy with his stopwatch. He wouldn't have had the time to melt the ice.

"What happened?" Jimmy asked, walking up to the group clustered around the melted ice sculpture.

Nan told him.

"We have to call off this event," Jimmy said. "There isn't enough time to finish before the judging tomorrow."

Mr. Mercer shook his head. "Don't worry," he said to the ice carvers. "We'll figure out something."

"How can we make a castle without a tower?" Nan asked.

"Make something else," Benny suggested.

"We'd better go check *our* sculpture," Violet said, and they all paraded over there. Violet's team's ice carving had not been damaged.

"That's a relief," she said.

Just then, Freddy and Beth ran to join them.

"What's up?" Henry asked.

Freddy raised her hand. In it was Benny's pink cup.

"Hey," Benny said, "what're you doing with my cup?"

"I found it at the rink, Benny," Freddy told him.

Benny's mouth dropped open. The last time he had seen his cup, his snow self was holding it.

"Someone's ruined the ice," Beth said. "Patches are chipped and broken. People trying to skate there would have trouble staying on their feet. Racing or figure skating would be impossible."

Freddy held up a chisel. "Whoever did it used this."

"Who could've done this?" Benny wondered aloud.

Beth and Freddy stared at him.

"Wait a minute," Benny said. "You don't think *I* did it?"

"Of course they don't, Benny," Jessie assured him.

Freddy held up the cup again. "Whoever

left this here wanted us to think you did it," she said and gave it to him.

All of a sudden, Jimmy said, "I'll see you later. I have to talk to Mr. Mercer. Maybe he'll call off the games." He dashed away.

Watching him, Freddy said, "He is really acting weird. I don't know how many times he's said we should call off the games."

Everyone headed toward the lodge.

"He probably just wants everything to go right," Beth said.

"With his parents coming for the awards dinner and everything," Jessie put in.

Freddy looked at her in disbelief. "His parents aren't coming for dinner," she said. "They never come for anything. They just drop him here. They don't even pick him up until everyone else has gone home."

"But he told us they were coming," Benny said.

"Wishful thinking," Freddy responded.

Matt rushed up. "My skis are back," he told them. "I just found them in the equipment shop."

"This is getting stranger and stranger," Freddy commented.

After dinner, Mr. Mercer clapped for silence. "As you all know, we've had some trouble this year," he said. "First the keys to the equipment shop were missing, then my tires were flat. Someone damaged the snow sculptures and one of the ice carvings." Then, he went on, "Jimmy Phelps came to talk to me at breakfast this morning. He thought we should call off the ski race because Matt's skis were missing."

Henry leaned toward Jessie. "Didn't Matt say he left the skis by the rack just before breakfast?" he whispered.

Jessie searched her memory. "I think so," she said.

"And he didn't know they were missing until the race?"

Jessie nodded.

"How did Jimmy know they were missing *at* breakfast?"

Her eyes wide, Jessie looked at her brother. Did he think Jimmy had caused all the trouble?

CHAPTER 15

# *The Solution*

"Now I've just learned that the ice at the rink has been ruined. But we're not going to cancel anything," Mr. Mercer said. Then he announced a new schedule. The ice-carving judging would be postponed. A crew was hosing the ice, and the skating competition would take place when it was ready. Sledding would be moved into its time slot.

"My message to whoever caused the trouble is this," Mr. Mercer concluded. "It won't work. Snow Haven Lodgers never quit!"

Everyone cheered.

Henry and Jessie were on their feet, ready to go.

"Come on," Henry urged Violet and Benny. "Let's go back to the cabin."

"But I haven't finished my cake," Benny protested.

Jessie pulled a paper napkin from the holder in the center of the table. "Wrap it in this," she said, "and bring it with you."

Grumbling, Benny did as he was told.

Henry and Jessie raced through the lounge with Violet and Benny trailing along behind.

Outside, Violet asked, "Why are we in such a hurry?"

"We have a new suspect," Henry told them.

"Not another one," Benny groaned. "There are already too many."

"But this might be the *right* one," Jessie said.

They wouldn't say another word until they were settled back at the cabin with a fire burning in the fireplace.

Then, Henry said, "So far the clues have pointed to Freddy and Pete."

"And all of us," Jessie added.

"Watch, too," Benny put in.

"We know it wasn't Watch or us," Violet said.

"It looks as if it wasn't Freddy or Pete either," Henry said.

Violet and Benny couldn't stand the suspense. "Then who was it?" they both asked.

"Violet, remember what you said?" Jessie asked. "That it might be someone we hadn't even thought about?"

Violet nodded.

"Well, you were right," Jessie said.

"It's the *last* person we would have thought," Henry added. He paused to let that sink in.

"Don't tell me it was Mr. Mercer!" Benny exclaimed.

They all laughed.

"No, no, Benny," Henry said. "Jessie and I think it was . . . Jimmy."

"Jimmy?" Benny repeated.

"But why?" Violet said.

Henry glanced at Jessie.

"Don't look at me, Henry," she said. "I

don't have the answer to that question."

"We'll leave the *why* till last," Henry decided. "Maybe it'll come to us as we answer the other questions."

"What made you think of Jimmy in the first place?" Violet wanted to know.

"He asked Mr. Mercer to cancel the ski race *at breakfast*," Henry explained, "but not even Matt knew his skis were missing until after lunch."

"The only way Jimmy could have known is if *he* took them," Violet concluded.

"What about our snowpeople?" Benny asked. "Freddy came late for supper. She had time to smash them."

"Jimmy was late, too," Jessie remembered.

"There's the ice sculpture," Violet said.

They fell silent trying to figure out when and how Jimmy could have done that.

Suddenly, Benny knew the answer. "The pail!" he said.

They looked at him curiously.

"Don't you remember? We were going for a snack and Jimmy came along carrying a pail."

"That's right," Jessie said. "He told us he'd found it by your snow sculpture, Benny."

"But Alan and Debbie brought our pails back to the kitchen," Benny said. "I'm sure of it."

"Jimmy must have carried hot water in it," Henry concluded. "He probably poured it on the ice castle to melt it."

"There's still the ice rink," Jessie reminded them.

"Everyone was too busy today to do much skating," Henry said. "Jimmy could've chopped up that ice any time."

"He left the ski hill after his turn," Benny said. "He probably did it then."

"Before he melted the castle," Jessie added.

"What about the missing keys?" Violet asked.

"And the flat tires?" Benny added.

"I'm not sure about those things," Henry said. "Jimmy did have the chance to do them, but — "

"That's right!" Benny interrupted. "Mr. Mercer said he parked the truck by the ice

rink. Jimmy went skating that morning —
before breakfast!"

"The keys disappeared the first day," Violet said. "Jimmy could have taken them
when he signed the guest book."

They decided to take a break from thinking. Jessie got out their homemade cookies
and poured juice. Benny unwrapped his
cake. They ate in silence.

Finally, Violet said, "I guess we've answered all the questions."

"Except the most important one," Henry
responded. "We still don't know *why* he did
it."

Jessie nodded her agreement. "The only
person who knows the answer to that is
Jimmy."

"Well, then," Benny said, "we'll have to
ask him."

CHAPTER 16

# The Motive

The children agreed to talk to Jimmy privately and ask him why he had tried to ruin the games. But, the next morning, Jimmy did not show up for breakfast. And no one had seen him.

"Maybe he's in his room," Benny said.

Henry asked Freddy for Jimmy's room number.

"I don't think he's there," Freddy said. "I knocked this morning. He didn't answer."

"Do you suppose he's sick?" Violet asked.

"There's only one way to find out," Henry replied.

The Aldens headed down the long lodge hall. They stopped before Jimmy's door.

Benny's idea had sounded simple. But now that they were about to face Jimmy, they were having second thoughts.

"What'll we say?" Benny whispered.

"We'll think of something," Henry said. He took a deep breath and knocked.

No answer.

He knocked again. "Jimmy?" he called. "It's Henry Alden."

"Ask if he's sick," Violet urged her brother.

"Are you all right, Jimmy?" Henry called.

Silence.

The Aldens stood quietly for several seconds.

"Maybe we should get Mr. Mercer," Violet whispered. "If Jimmy's sick, he might need help."

They turned to leave. The door opened slowly. Jimmy peeked out. He looked pale. Even his cheeks had lost their rosy color.

"Oh, Jimmy," Jessie said. "You weren't at breakfast; we thought you might be sick."

"I — uh — just wasn't . . . hungry," Jimmy said.

"Then you *must* be sick," Benny commented.

That made everyone — even Jimmy — smile.

"We'd like to talk to you," Henry said. "About the games."

At first, Jimmy was silent. Then, he said, "Come on in."

They followed him into his room.

Henry cleared his throat. "We've been trying to figure out who's responsible for all that's happened," he began.

"We thought it might be Freddy or Pete," Jessie added.

"So their team could win," Benny said.

"But then their own ice carving was melted," Violet said.

"I did it." Jimmy's voice was so quiet the Aldens weren't certain they'd heard it.

After a brief silence, Henry said, "You did?"

Jimmy sank down on the edge of his bed. "All of it," he said.

Benny nodded. "We thought so," he said.

"You planted Freddy's glove and hat?" Henry asked.

Jimmy nodded.

"And Pete's earmuffs?" Jessie asked.

Jimmy nodded again.

"And my cup?" Benny wanted to know.

"Yes," Jimmy told him.

"That's what was so confusing," Henry said. "There were so many suspects."

"I didn't want anyone to take the blame," Jimmy explained. "First, I took the keys and let the air out of the tires. I didn't leave clues then. I thought that would be enough. Mr. Mercer would stop the games. But it didn't work."

"Why did you want the games stopped?" Jessie asked.

Jimmy sighed deeply. After a long pause, he began, "I've been coming here for years. Alone." He paused again to take a deep breath. "It was my idea to begin with. I was six or seven. I thought it'd be neat, you know, to be . . . on my own. And it was fun. I liked it a lot. But it got to be a regular thing. Every year, my parents would drop me here and go to some other place." He rarely saw his parents, Jimmy told them. Mr. and Mrs. Phelps were busy lawyers. Now Jimmy wanted to spend vacation with them. If the Snow Haven winter games were canceled, maybe they'd start taking him along with them.

"Have you ever told them how you feel?" Violet asked softly.

"No," Jimmy admitted. "They're my parents; they should *know* how I feel."

"They're not mind readers," Henry said.

"Even if I did tell them, they wouldn't care," Jimmy argued.

Benny sat down beside Jimmy. "That's what we thought about our grandfather," he said.

Jimmy looked surprised. "Mr. Alden is a terrific man."

"But we didn't know that at first," Violet said.

Henry told Jimmy about their days in the

boxcar and their fear of a grandfather they didn't even know.

"We learned our lesson," Jessie said. "Now, we say what's on our minds."

Jimmy smiled. "Benny didn't need that lesson," he teased. "I bet he was born saying what was on his mind."

Everybody laughed.

Then, Jimmy grew serious again. "Maybe you're right. Maybe it's not all their fault. Maybe it's mine, too." He looked at the Aldens. "But what can I do about it?"

They all thought about that.

Finally, Jessie said, "Why don't you call them?"

"That's a good idea," Henry agreed.

"You mean *now*?" Jimmy sounded uncertain.

"The sooner the better," Jessie said.

Jimmy got to his feet. "All right," he said. "I'll do it. But first, will you come with me to talk to Mr. Mercer?"

The Aldens understood. It would be difficult to tell Mr. Mercer what he had done; he needed support.

# CHAPTER 17

# The Winners

Mr. Mercer took them into his small office. There, Jimmy gave Mr. Mercer the equipment shop keys. Then, he told his story. The man sat silently, listening.

"It was a dumb thing to do," Jimmy concluded. "And I'm really sorry. I'll do anything I can to make up for it."

Mr. Mercer nodded. For a long time, he didn't say a word. He just kept nodding. The room was so quiet Jimmy and the Aldens could hear themselves breathing.

Finally, Mr. Mercer said, "Telling me this has not been easy." He paused. "I think we'll just keep it to ourselves." He glanced at Jimmy. "Is that all right with you?"

"Oh, yes, sir," Jimmy replied. The color came back to his cheeks.

"Fine. Now go on out of here, all of you." Mr. Mercer turned his chair toward his desk. "I have work to do."

They started out.

"Oh, Jimmy, there is one thing you can do," Mr. Mercer said.

"Anything, sir," Jimmy responded.

"For the remainder of the games, I expect you to do your best — like the champion you are."

Jimmy smiled broadly. "You can count on it," he said.

He went back to his room to phone his parents. The Aldens waited for him in the lounge.

"Maybe Jimmy's parents will change their minds and come for the awards dinner," Jessie said.

"I hope so," Violet said.

Jimmy came toward them. His eyes were sad.

Benny was surprised to see him back so soon. "You didn't talk very long," he said.

"I didn't talk at all," Jimmy replied. "They weren't there."

"Maybe they're out to breakfast," Violet said.

Jimmy shook his head. "They've checked out of the hotel. No one knows where they went."

At last it was time for the judging of the ice carvings. Watch sat very still beside his ice self.

"He wants everyone to know he posed for it," Benny said.

Nan's group had turned their ice castle into a dog house. Watch's name was carved on the door.

The judges called it a tie.

The next two days were busy.

As he had promised, Jimmy did his best in the remaining events. Everyone else did well, too.

Everything was more fun. The lounge was always full of people playing word games and talking. The teams mixed more freely. Benny did very well in his sledding race, and afterwards, everyone — even the adults — had a gigantic snowball fight. No one won. But it didn't seem to matter.

Skating was the last event. It was held on the afternoon of the awards dinner. Once more, the ice was smooth as glass. Beth and Jessie did figure skating dances. Jimmy and Matt raced against Freddy and another member of her team. All the skaters took part in the last race, a relay.

The crowd roared as the baton was passed from one person to the next. It was the closest, most exciting race of the week. Only Pete and his stopwatch seemed to know who had won. And he wasn't telling.

Back at the lodge, people talked about the games.

Jimmy stood by the fire, talking with the Aldens. "This was probably the best — " He broke off. The smile froze on his face.

"What's the matter?" Henry asked.

Jimmy didn't say a word. He just kept staring.

The Aldens followed his gaze. Standing inside the door were Mr. and Mrs. Phelps!

Jimmy sprang into action. "Mom! Dad!" he called and sprinted across the room to meet them.

Mrs. Phelps hugged her son. Mr. Phelps hugged him, too.

"I called you," Jimmy told them. "You'd checked out."

"We decided to surprise you," Mr. Phelps said.

Jimmy took them over by the fire. "These are my friends," he said and introduced the Aldens.

"No wonder you like it here, Jimmy," Mr. Phelps said. "There are so many interesting people."

"The whole time we were away, we kept wishing we were here with you," Mrs. Phelps said.

Jimmy couldn't hide his surprise. "And I was wishing I was there with you," he told them. After that, all his feelings came tumbling out.

The Phelps were stunned. They had always thought he wanted to come here for the winter games. And they thought he liked being on his own.

"What a terrible misunderstanding!" Mrs. Phelps said.

"From now on, we'll discuss these things," Mr. Phelps said. "And the next time we take a vacation, it will be together."

Mrs. Phelps glanced around the room. She seemed to like what she saw. "And maybe we'll spend it at Snow Haven," she said.

"That'd be great," Benny put in. "We might be here, too."

The parade into the dining room began. Mr. Alden stood at the door beside Mr. Mercer.

"Well, Benny, are you ready to eat?" Mr. Alden asked.

"I'm too excited to eat," Benny said. "I can't wait until we find out who won."

Mr. Mercer laughed. "I'll save you the suspense, Benny," he said. "In my book, you're all winners."

GERTRUDE CHANDLER WARNER discovered when she was teaching that many readers who like an exciting story could find no books that were both easy and fun to read. She decided to try to meet this need, and her first book, *The Boxcar Children*, quickly proved she had succeeded.

Miss Warner drew on her own experiences to write each mystery. As a child she spent hours watching trains go by on the tracks opposite her family home. She often dreamed about what it would be like to set up housekeeping in a caboose or freight car — the situation the Alden children find themselves in.

When Miss Warner received requests for more adventures involving Henry, Jessie, Violet, and Benny Alden, she began additional stories. In each, she chose a special setting and introduced unusual or eccentric characters who liked the unpredictable.

While the mystery element is central to each of Miss Warner's books, she never thought of them as strictly juvenile mysteries. She liked to stress the Aldens' independence and resourcefulness and their solid New England devotion to using up and making do. The Aldens go about most of their adventures with as little adult supervision as possible — something else that delights young readers.

Miss Warner lived in Putnam, Connecticut, until her death in 1979. During her lifetime, she received hundreds of letters from girls and boys telling her how much they liked her books.